THE TWELVE LABOURS

1. **This book may be kept three weeks. It is to be returned on / before the last date stamped below.**
2. **A fine of 20p will be charged for every week or part of week a book is overdue.**

// JAN 2003

For Zocia

THE TWELVE LABOURS OF HERACLES

ECHO AND NARCISSUS

GERALDINE M^CCAUGHREAN
ILLUSTRATED BY TONY ROSS

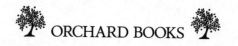

ORCHARD BOOKS

ORCHARD BOOKS
96 Leonard Street, London EC2A 4RH
Orchard Books Australia
14 Mars Road, Lane Cove, NSW 2066
ISBN 1 86039 437 X (hardback)
ISBN 1 86039 530 9 (paperback)
First published in Great Britain 1997
Text © Geraldine McCaughrean 1992
Illustrations © Tony Ross 1997
1 2 3 4 5 6 02 01 00 99 98 97
The right of Geraldine McCaughrean to be identified as the
author and Tony Ross as the illustrator of this
work has been asserted by them in accordance with the
Copyright, Designs and Patents Act, 1988.
A CIP catalogue record for this book is available from the
British Library.
Printed in Great Britain

THE TWELVE
LABOURS OF
HERACLES

There was once a baby born who was so remarkable that the gods themselves stared down at his cradle. He was called Heracles, and when huge snakes slithered into his crib to strangle him, he knotted and plaited them as if they were pieces of string, and threw them out again.

For Heracles was strong—
fantastically strong—stronger than you
and me and a hundred others put
together. Fortunately, he was also gentle
and kind, so that his friends had
nothing to fear from him. His
schoolteacher made him promise never
to touch alcoholic drink, though. "If
you were ever to get drunk, Heracles,"
the schoolmaster said, "who knows
what terrible thing you might do with
that great strength of yours!"

Heracles promised, and he truly
meant to keep his promise. But then his
friends all drank at parties, his family
always had wine with their meals: it
seemed foolish for Heracles to ask for

fruit juice or water. So he was tempted
to take just one glass of wine—and
after that another—and another—and
another. Soon he was roaring drunk,
throwing punches in all directions.
When the wine's work was done,
Heracles' own family lay
dead on the floor,
and Heracles was
an outcast hated by
everyone and most
of all by himself.

For his crime, he was condemned to
serve King Eurystheus as a slave for
seven years. Eurystheus was a mean,
spiteful man—whose kingdom was
overrun by a great many problems—

and he decided to set Heracles the twelve most dangerous tasks he could think of—tasks that were to become known as the Twelve Labours of Heracles.

A giant lion was terrorising his kingdom, eating men, women and children. "Go and kill the lion, slave," he told Heracles.

Heracles was so miserable that he did not much care whether he lived or died. He found the lion's den and strode in, with no weapon but his bare hands. When the beast sprang at him, Heracles took it by the throat and shook it like a rug, then wrung it out like washing. When it was dead, he skinned it and wore the lion skin for a tunic, knotting the paws around his waist and shoulders.

If King Eurystheus was grateful, he did not show it, but simply set Heracles his Second Labour, "If you can kill lions," he said, "you may as well try to kill the hydra."

The Hydra was a water serpent which lived in the middle of a swamp. When it was born, it had nine heads. But each time one was cut off, two new heads grew to replace it. By the time Heracles came face to face with the Hydra, it had fifty heads, all gnashing their horrible teeth.

Heracles was quick with his sword and nimble on his feet. But though he slashed through many snaking necks without being bitten, the struggle only became more difficult. The heads just multiplied! So Heracles ran off a short way and lit a fire. Then he heated his wooden club red-hot and, with his sword in one hand and his club in the other, he re-entered the fight.

This time, as he cut through each neck, he singed the ragged end with his red-hot club, and the head did not regrow. At last the Hydra looked like nothing more than a knobbly tree stump

There was no time to rest after fighting the Hydra. King Eurystheus sent him to capture a stag with golden antlers, then to kill a huge wild boar.

Heracles' fifth Labour was a particularly unpleasant one: to clean the Augean stables.

Lord Augeas kept one thousand animals penned up in sties and stables stretching the length of a foul valley. He was too idle to clean out his animals and too mean to hire farmhands. So the wretched beasts stood up to their bellies in dung. People for miles around complained about the smell.

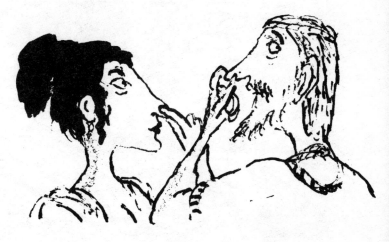

Heracles stood on a hilltop, looking down on the valley, holding his nose. He saw a river bubbling close by, and it gave him an idea. Moving boulders as easily as if they were feather pillows, he built a dam, so that the river flowed out of its course and down the valley instead. Startled horses and cows and

goats and sheep staggered in a torrent of rushing water, but the dung beneath them was scoured away by the river. Heracles only had to demolish the dam with one blow of his club, and the river flowed back to its old river bed. The animals stood shivering and shaking themselves dry, in a green, clean valley.

King Eurystheus was ready and
waiting with his
next three
commands.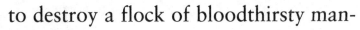
Heracles was
to destroy a flock of bloodthirsty man-

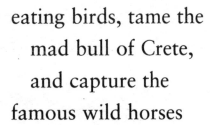

eating birds, tame the
mad bull of Crete,
and capture the
famous wild horses

which could run faster than the wind.

By now the king had begun to feel very
nervous of his slave. He had a big

bronze vase made and hid inside it whenever Heracles came back from doing his work.

"The mad bull is tamed, master. The man-eating birds are now dead, and your wild horses are outside in the yard," said Heracles, when he returned soon after. "What must I do next?"

But Eurystheus was running out of problems and his mind turned to thoughts of getting rich with the help of Heracles.

"Get me the jewelled belt worn by the Queen of the Amazons!" said the king, from inside his urn.

Here was one task for which Heracles did not mean to use his great strength. He simply went to the queen

of those savage female warriors and explained why he was there. She took an instant liking to him and gave him the belt straight away. Unfortunately, word spread through the camp that Heracles had come to kill the queen and he had to fight a thousand angry women, fierce as wasps, before he could escape with the jewelled belt.

And so it continued. No sooner did
Heracles finish one task, than he was set
another one. To fetch King Eurystheus
the legendary giant oxen, Heracles
made a bridge over the sea
by bending
two mountain
peaks out
across the
water. To fetch
Pluto's three-

headed dog, Cerberus, he travelled down
to the fearful Underworld.

But the twelfth and last and greediest
of the king's commands was for
Heracles to bring him the apples of the
Hesperides. These magical fruit grew
on a tree in a garden at the end of the
world, and around that tree coiled a
dragon which never slept.

Even Heracles, with all his courage and strength, quailed at the thought of fighting the dragon. Better by far that a friend should ask it for the fruit and be allowed to take them. So Heracles went to see a giant named Atlas.

Now Atlas was no ordinary giant, as big as a house. Atlas was the biggest man in the world, and towered above houses, trees, cliffs and hills. He was so tall that the gods had given him the task of holding up the sky and keeping

the stars from falling. The sun scorched
his neck and the new moon shaved his
beard. And for thousands of years he
had stood in the one spot.

"How can I go to the end of the world?" said Atlas, when Heracles asked him for the favour. "How can I go anywhere?"

"I could hold the sky for you while you were gone," suggested Heracles..

"Could you? Would you? Then I'll do it!" said Atlas.

So Heracles took the sky on his
back—though it was the heaviest
burden he had ever carried. Atlas
stretched himself, then strode away
towards the end of the world: the
gardeners were members of his family.

Fetching the apples was no hardship. But as the giant hurried back across the world, carrying the precious fruit, he thought how wonderful it felt to be free! As he got closer to home, the thought of carrying that weight of sky seemed less and less attractive. His steps slowed. When at last he reached Heracles—poor exhausted, bone-bent Heracles—Atlas exclaimed, "I've decided! I'm going to let you go on holding up the sky, and I'll deliver these apples to King Eurystheus."

again—just while Heracles made a pad for his shoulders. He even gave Heracles the apples to hold because he needed both hands.

"Well, I'll be on my way now," said Heracles, juggling with the apples as he scurried away. "Most grateful for your help. Perhaps next time, you'll get the better of me."

After seven years, Heracles' hard labours came to an end, and he was free. But he was never free from his sorrow at taking that first glass of wine: not until the day he died.

Being only a man and not a god, he did die. But the gods did not forget him. They cut him out in stars and hung him in the sky, to rest from his labours for all time, among the singing planets.

ECHO AND
NARCISSUS

All the goddesses liked to run through the silent woods on Mount Olympus, playing and chasing the deer. There was Queen Hera, soundless as the sun's rays; there was Diana, quiet as moonlight; there were the wood nymphs flitting like thistledown ... and then there was Echo.

Echo was always chattering, arguing or shrieking with laughter. The deer scattered as soon as Echo opened her mouth.

"Echo!" said Hera sternly to her one day. "You've done it again!"

"What? Didn't do anything," said Echo pertly.

"Yes you did. You talked. You're always talking."

"I'm not!"

"You are. Don't tell me you're not."

"Not," said Echo, who always had to have the last word. "Not, not, not."

Hera was so angry that she pointed a magic finger at Echo. "Once and for all, be silent!"

The nymph was struck dumb. She put her hands to her throat, her fingers to her lips, and looked around in horror.

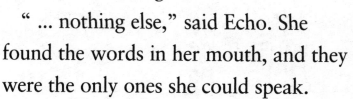

"Let this be a lesson to you. You always wanted the last word. Now you shall have nothing else!"

" ... nothing else," said Echo. She found the words in her mouth, and they were the only ones she could speak.

"You may go now," said the queen of the gods.

" ... go now," said Echo, without meaning to.

Echo ran
sobbing off
the mountain
and wandered
about miserably
in the foothills.
There, amid
his flock of

sheep, she saw a shepherd boy. He was

combing his
curly hair
into ringlets
and brushing
the grass off
his tunic.
This was
Narcissus,

and Narcissus was as beautiful as any god. The shepherdesses could not lay eyes on him without falling in love.

Echo was no different from the shepherdesses. She fell in love with Narcissus at first sight, and what she would have given to be able to tell him so! But her lips were sealed like a locked door. All she could do was follow him about, her hands full of flowers and her eyes full of love.

"What can I do for you?" he asked, when he saw her gazing at him.

" ... for you ...," said Echo, and laid the flowers at his feet.

Unfortunately, Narcissus was quite used to women falling in love with him. It happened all the time. He knew how handsome he was and that made him very, very vain. Worse still, he did not much like women, did not want their sickly, syrupy love. Echo only annoyed him, trailing along behind him, saying nothing, staring with her mouth open.

"Everywhere I go, you follow," he complained.

" ... follow ... follow," said Echo.

"Stupid girl, I suppose you think you love me."

" ... love me ... love me," pleaded Echo

"You bore me. Leave me alone!"

" ... alone! alone!" wailed Echo. The word filled her with horror.

Day after week after month she dogged Narcissus' footsteps. In her unhappiness she grew pale and thin, and when all her beauty had faded because of her love for him, he said,

"Oh do go away! I hate the sight of you. Do you really suppose I could ever care for a stick-insect like you? Look at yourself!"

"Look at yourself! ... Look at yourself!" sobbed Echo.

"Gladly," said the vain young man, and went to the pool in the centre of the forest and examined his reflection.

Echo's love turned to hate, and though she had no words, she wished a wicked, wordless wish. She wished that Narcissus should one day love as she loved him, and suffer for it as she was suffering.

Then she wandered away into the forest where in her misery, she grew thinner and thinner, paler and paler.

At last her body faded away altogether. Only her voice was left to blow about with the leaves.

All this while, Narcissus sat by the pool staring at his reflection. Somehow he could not seem to tear himself away. The more he looked, the more he liked what he saw. Narcissus fell in love with the face in the water, just as Echo had fallen in love with him. He longed to kiss those lips, just as Echo had longed to kiss his.

At last, leaning down towards the shining pool, he kissed the water—and the face reflected there dissolved into ripples.

"Oh don't go!" Narcissus reached out and plunged his hand into the water, but only managed to shatter the reflection altogether. So he sat very still and gazed and gazed and gazed ...

Meanwhile, in her palace, Hera, queen of the gods, regretted her temper and sent her handmaidens to look for Echo and forgive her. They searched the high rocks and wooded places, but when they called her name—"Echo! Echo!" —their words simply floated back to them on the breeze: "... Echo!... Echo!"

They did find one thing, though—a pretty yellow and white flower growing beside a pond. It leaned out over the water as if admiring its own reflection.

For Narcissus had taken root where he sat. He too had pined away in hopeless love, until all that remained of his body were tissuey petals and a bending stalk.

"I've never seen this kind of flower before," said one of the nymphs. "I wonder what it's called."

And the breeze in the woods seemed to whisper, "Narcissus! Narcissus!"

To this day, the same flower can be found growing wild on the banks of ponds, leaning out over the water as if in love with its own reflection. And people call it narcissus, though they have long since forgotten the vain shepherd boy.